POPSICLE PONY

POPSICLE

**For Johnny, Jeannine, and David
who were there all the time**

Lothrop, Lee & Shepard Books, a division of
William Morrow & Company, Inc., 1350
Avenue of the Americas, New York, New
York 10019. Printed in Singapore.
First Edition   1 2 3 4 5 6 7 8 9 10
Library of Congress Cataloging in
Publication data was not available in
time for publication of this book.
ISBN 0-688-12392-9   ISBN 0-688-12393-7
(lib. bdg.)   Library of Congress Catalog
Card Number 93-79774

PONY

JILL STOVER

LOTHROP, LEE & SHEPARD BOOKS   NEW YORK

When I was little, there weren't any fancy ice-cream trucks like there are now. But there *was* Popsicle Pete, who sold Popsicles from a wagon pulled by his pony,

Chiefy. Every hot summer evening I waited for them
on the porch. For a dime I could buy whatever flavor I
wanted—orange or cherry or grape or lime.

Chiefy was a stubborn pony, but Popsicle Pete knew just how to handle him. They always took the same

route through town. First they went by the Moo-Moo
to pick up the Popsicles. Chiefy got a special treat.

Next they went past the Longhorn Feed Store,

and Chiefy got another little something.

Then they stopped at the Twin Dolphins Movie Theater,

where Chiefy got one more snack.

Finally they trotted on past the jail and the hospital and around the corner to my house.

We could hear the clip-clop of Chiefy's hooves as we waited.

Sometimes Popsicle Pete let us climb into the chariot,
and Chiefy would let me sit on his back.

Then we would all ride around the block in the twilight.

One evening Popsicle Pete didn't come. He was sick and had to go to the hospital for a few days. Chiefy came to stay with me. My backyard became a real Texas ranch, and I turned into a real Texas cowgirl.

Chiefy needed food and water and grooming, and I had big plans to ride him in the county fair parade. We only had a week to practice.

Every morning I tried to ride Chiefy over to the hospital to see Popsicle Pete. And every morning he refused to go. I coaxed him with carrots. I bribed him with

cookies. I even tried chili peppers. But Chiefy was stubborn, and I didn't know how to handle him. He wouldn't budge.

On the morning of the parade, I went out to try one
more time. The yard was empty. Chiefy had escaped.

Pretty soon we got a call from the county sheriff. Chiefy
was in big trouble.

After his great escape, he had taken his regular route through town. First he went to the Moo-Moo to get a special treat. Then he went past the Longhorn Feed Store for another little something.

Finally he stopped at the Twin Dophins Movie Theater
for one more snack. The movie must have been pretty
exciting, because Chiefy decided to stay. But he raised
a ruckus, and the manager called in the sheriff.

When he was arrested, Chiefy trotted happily along his regular route to the county jail, where he was locked in a cell to keep him out of any more trouble.

I went down to pick him up. On our way home I had an
idea. *Now* I knew how to handle Chiefy.

I polished my boots and put on my new parade dress
and gussied up the little pony.

Then I hitched him to Popsicle Pete's wagon and led him downtown where the parade was set to begin.

I climbed onto Chiefy's back and he knew just what to
do. He pranced to the head of the parade. Then he led
all of the horses to the Moo-Moo, where they each got
a special treat.

Next he led them to the Longhorn Feed Store, where they got another little something. Then he led them to the Twin Dolphins Movie Theater, where they each got one more snack.

The whole parade followed Chiefy along Popsicle Pete's route. As we passed the hospital, Popsicle Pete waved from his window.

Chiefy saluted him proudly.

Then he clip-clopped around the corner into my backyard.

4/28/94